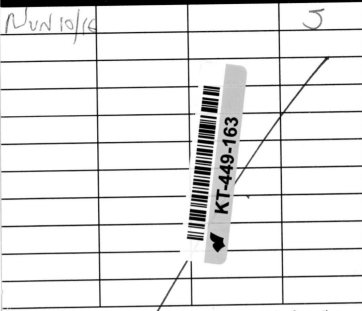

FURRY FRIENDS

Sophie's Squeaky Surprise

HOLLY WEBB

Illustrated by Clare Elsom

SCHOLASTIC

For Eva and Phoebe

With huge thanks to Annie —
we must go back to Paris!

First published in 2016 by Scholastic Children's Books
An imprint of Scholastic Ltd
Euston House, 24 Eversholt Street, London, NW1 1DB, UK
Registered office: Westfield Road, Southam, Warwickshire, CV47 0RA
SCHOLASTIC and associated logos are trademarks and/or
registered trademarks of Scholastic Inc.

Text copyright © Holly Webb, 2016
Illustration copyright © Clare Elsom, 2016

The rights of Holly Webb and Clare Elsom to be identified
as the author and illustrator of this work have been asserted by them.

ISBN 978 1407 15432 9

A CIP catalogue record for this book
is available from the British Library.

Printed by CPI Group (UK) Ltd, Croydon, CR0 4YY

Papers used by Scholastic Children's Books are made
from wood grown in sustainable forests.

1 3 5 7 9 10 8 6 4 2

This is a work of fiction. Names, characters, places, incidents
and dialogues are products of the author's imagination or are used
fictitiously. Any resemblance to actual people, living or dead,
events or locales is entirely coincidental.

www.scholastic.co.uk

In a great big city, in the middle of
France, is a church that stands on a hill.

The church is white, with a dome
on the top, and it looks like a wedding
cake. It's a very old church, and very
famous, so every day lots of people come
to visit.

They tell each other how
pretty it is, and then they
notice the steep steps
that go up to the
top of the hill,
and they sigh.

Those steps really are *very* steep.

But once the visitors have got to the top, they turn round to see a beautiful view of the city of Paris. You can see so far across the city, and there are so many roofs and towers and glittering domes to look at, that most of them forget how much their knees hurt.

The view is so beautiful that hardly any of the visitors look back at the steep grass slope, and the steps they've climbed. They never think about what's underneath.

Or who...

Only a very few people ever find out, and this is *their* story.

CHAPTER ONE

Sophie peered out over the view, watching the sunlight sparkle on the windows, and wondering who lived there, under the roofs. She couldn't see her own house from here, or she didn't think she could, anyway. She hadn't lived in Paris for long enough to know.

The city *was* very beautiful, but it still
didn't feel like home. Sophie sighed, and
rested her chin on her hands. She missed
her old house, and her old bedroom, and
her cat, Oscar. Grandma was looking

after him while they lived in Paris, but Sophie was sure that Oscar missed her, almost as much as she missed him.

"What are you looking at?" Dan squashed up next to her, leaning over the stone balcony.

"Just things," Sophie said vaguely. "The view."

"Boring," Dan muttered. "This is taking ages. And I'm hungry." He turned round, holding his tummy in both hands and made a starving face at Sophie. His nose scrunched up like a rabbit's, and Sophie smirked. She crossed her eyes and poked her tongue out at the corner of her mouth to make Dan laugh. After all,

even a wonderful view can be boring
when you've been looking at it for a
VERY LONG TIME.

All the people who live in Paris love
their city so much, and many of them
walk up the steep steps to the church
on their wedding days to have their
photographs taken next to the wonderful
view. But it can take an awful long time
to get the photographs right, especially
when it's windy and your auntie's
wedding dress won't stay still properly.

"Sophie and Dan! Stop making faces
like that! You're making Dad giggle,
and he's supposed to be taking romantic
photos!" Mum glared at them, but Dad

rolled his eyes, and stuck his tongue out at Dan. Sophie thought Dad might be a bit bored with the photos as well.

This church was one of Sophie's favourite places in Paris. It was so pretty, and there was the fountain to look at, and all the people. She even liked its name, *Sacré Coeur*, which meant Sacred Heart. Sophie thought it was very special to have a whole church that was all about love. Auntie Lou's wedding had been beautiful too, but Sophie had got up early for Mum to curl her hair and fuss over her dress, and she was tired of having to stand still and smile.

"Go and play," Auntie Lou suggested.

"Go and run around for a bit. You can come back and be in the photos later."

"Later?" Dad moaned. "I thought we'd nearly finished!" But Sophie and Dan were already halfway down the white marble steps, and couldn't hear him.

"I wish we'd brought a ball..." Dan said, as they stopped in front of the fountain that stood below the balcony. He was looking at the grassy slope of the hill. "Do you think Mum would mind if we went home and got one? It wouldn't take five minutes."

"Yes, she would! And anyway, even *you* couldn't play football on that grass," Sophie pointed out. "It would just roll down to the bottom."

"Exactly. That would make it more fun! Uphill football, I've just invented it. I might be famous!"

Sophie shook her head. "I don't think all the people taking photos would be very impressed either. There are loads of them. They'd tell you off."

"Huh." But Dan looked round at all the visitors, and realized Sophie was right. No one looked as if they wanted to play football. And there was an old lady sitting on the bench over there with a really pointy umbrella, the kind with a parrot's head handle. She looked like she'd happily use the pointy end to stab footballs, and even the parrot seemed to be giving him a fierce glare.

"Race you up and down the balustrades then!" He grabbed her hand and hurried her down the two flights of stairs to the path.

Sophie squirmed. The balustrades were the stone slopes at the sides of the steps. They were wide and flat, and Dan loved to run up and down them. He'd discovered the game the first time they came to visit the church, just after they'd moved to Paris, and since *Sacré Coeur* was on their way home from school, he'd been practising. But the game made Sophie feel sick, especially when it had been raining and the stone was all slick and slippery. She was sure that he would fall off.

"Come on, Sophie!" Dan hopped up to the stonework. "You get up on the other side. Bet I can beat you back to the top!"

Sophie stood on the bottom step, looking anxiously at the flat white slope. She didn't want to run up it – but if she refused, Dan would keep on and on teasing her.

"Baby!" her brother called scornfully, and Sophie scowled. She was only a year younger than Dan! She was not a baby! Carefully, the tip of her tongue sticking out between her teeth, she stepped on to the balustrade. It wasn't really so very high, after all... And Dan looked so surprised that she'd done it! Sophie grinned at him.

"Go!" Dan yelled, dashing away up the slope. Sophie gasped, and raced after him, wishing she had trainers on, and not her best shoes with the glittery bows.

She slithered a little, and gasped and reached out her hands to balance, wishing there was something to hold on to – a tree maybe. But there was only the perfect short green grass, and every so often those funny little cone-shaped bushes that almost looked like upside-down ice creams.

Halfway to the top, Dan let out a yell as he spotted one of his friends from school on the other side of the hill. He hopped down and raced across the grass to see Benjamin, leaving Sophie glaring after him. He'd just abandoned their race, after she'd been brave enough to climb the balustrade at last. How could he? She folded her arms and tapped her foot crossly on the stone. Brothers! They were so rude!

If only she had a friend to play with, too. It wasn't fair. Sophie watched Dan

and Benjamin chasing each other across
the grass, and sighed sadly. Somehow,
she just hadn't found anybody she liked
that much at school yet. Even though
Mum had spoken French to them ever
since they were little, Sophie still felt
as though she wasn't doing it quite
right. The teachers told her she was
doing ever so well, but the girls in
her class looked at her funny whenever
she opened her mouth. And then they
just ran off. After some days at school,
Sophie wondered if she might forget
how to talk at all. It was nothing
like back home. Mum had suggested
sending emails to her friends from their

school in London, and Sophie had, but it wasn't the same at all. All the fun things that Elizabeth and Zara told her in their replies only made Sophie feel more left out.

The only girls who'd really spoken to her were Chloe and Adrienne, and that was because their teacher had asked them to look after the new girl. Sophie had decided halfway through the first morning that she'd much rather be unlooked-after. Chloe didn't do anything except twitch her nose and giggle, which was boring, though bearable, but Sophie thought

Adrienne was possibly the nastiest person she had ever met. Because her voice was so sweet and soft, the things she said sounded perfectly nice at first. It was only when Sophie thought back that she realized how horrible they actually were.

"So, why *did* you move here?" Adrienne had a way of looking at Sophie with her head on one side that made Sophie feel like she was some ugly sort of beetle.

"Your French is quite good. For an English person, I mean..."

"I suppose that's an *English* skirt. It's very ... interesting."

Sophie gave a little shiver, even though the sun was warm on her bare shoulders. It was a hot September afternoon, but Adrienne's pretty voice was like cold water trickling down her spine, even when she was only remembering it.

She sighed again, and then shuddered as Dan and Benjamin started a race, rolling down the grassy slope.

And then she fell off.

Afterwards, Sophie wasn't quite sure how she did it. She hadn't even been moving. But her feet seemed to slip suddenly from underneath her, and then her arms were flapping uselessly at the air. There was a thump, and she was flat

on the grass on her tummy, next to one
of those strange little cone-shaped bushes.

Sophie lay there, gasping and trying
not to cry. She wanted Dan to come and
pick her up – but at the same time she
didn't want him knowing she'd been silly
enough to fall.

"Are you all right?"

It wasn't Dan. The mystery voice was
speaking in French, and Dan would have
spoken to her in English. It just didn't
sound like Dan, anyway. Sophie hoped
it wasn't the old lady with the parrot
umbrella. She would probably say it
was all Sophie's own fault, and insist on
taking her back to Mum and Dad and

Auntie Lou and the endless photographs.

But surely even a very little old lady wouldn't have such a high, squeaky voice?

Sophie turned her head slightly, and squeaked herself.

Staring at her worriedly was a tiny furry face, ginger-and-white, with neat little ears, and shining eyes.

"Are you hurt?" the squeaky voice said again, and this time there was no doubt about it. It was definitely this small furry person who was talking to her.

"No, I'm not. Thank you for asking,"

Sophie whispered, trying to sit up.

"Oh, good. Yes, that's right. Much better." The guinea pig – for now that she was the right way up, Sophie could see that's what the furry little person was – nodded approvingly. "You didn't hit your head?"

"I don't think so," Sophie murmured, shaking it gently. Though if she had bumped her head, it would explain why she was talking to a guinea pig. And, more importantly, how the guinea pig seemed to be talking back.

"Are you imaginary?" she asked, wondering if she had actually hit her head *very hard*.

"Certainly not!" The guinea pig's voice became even squeakier. Sophie was surprised it could manage it. "Whatever gave you that idea?" it asked indignantly.

"Well. You're talking. And ... and you've got a pink ballet skirt on."

The guinea pig looked down at her middle – now she'd noticed the skirt, Sophie was guessing that the guinea pig was probably a girl. Then she flounced the skirt with her little pink paws and did a twirl, gazing at her plump middle with a great deal of satisfaction. "I know. I found it yesterday. Do you like it? I think it suits me very well. But I suppose you haven't seen that many guinea pigs wearing clothes

before. I can see why you'd be surprised."

"Actually, my friend Elizabeth from home is always trying to dress up her hamster," Sophie admitted. "But he bites her, every time. It was really the talking that seemed so unusual."

"Oh..." The guinea pig looked faintly worried, and her tiny round ears twitched. "It's just possible that I shouldn't have spoken to you. It *is* meant to be a secret, actually. But I was frightened that you were hurt. You were lying so still. I'm sure the others will understand." She smoothed the pink net of her skirt with anxious little pats of her paws.

"I promise I won't tell anybody," Sophie said quickly. "It was very nice of you to be worried about me." Then she frowned. "But if you're supposed to be a secret, should you be standing there like that? Everyone can see you."

The guinea pig let out a panicked

breath of a squeak. "Mercy me! I haven't even got my hat on! Do excuse me a moment." She whisked round, and disappeared under the little cone-shaped bush in a blur of ginger fur and shocking-pink net.

A minute later she was back, with a neat circle of grass attached to the top of her head. It was held on with a green ribbon, tied in a large bow under her chin.

"We'll be all right now," the guinea pig told Sophie. "Thank you for noticing, I can't think how I came to be so careless. I'll forget my own name next. It's Josephine," she added. "I didn't tell

you, did I?" She
bobbed Sophie
a little curtsey,
holding out the
ballet skirt with
her paws.

Sophie looked
around nervously. She
wasn't sure that the grassy hat was
actually enough of a disguise. The
guinea pig still looked very much like
a guinea pig, except that now she had
long green tufty hair. There were people
climbing the stone steps past them all the
time. She wondered if she should offer to
let the guinea pig hide under the edge of

her skirt. "It's very nice to meet you. I'm Sophie. But..."

"I promise..." A little pink paw was resting on Sophie's lap. "No one will see. We've been here for so many years, you know. And no one ever does notice us. After all, it's such a silly story! A family of guinea pigs living underneath the beautiful church of *Sacré Coeur*? No one would ever believe it!"

"But I can see you," Sophie pointed out.

"Ah, if you're clever enough to see what I really am, you're clever enough to know that you must never, ever tell." Josephine's sparkling black eyes gazed hopefully into Sophie's blue ones, and Sophie nodded.

"Of course I won't. Unless ... I'm not very good at keeping secrets from Dan. He's my brother. I will if I have to, though."

"Hmmm. Well. A brother might be all right," Josephine said cautiously. "I shall have to see him first, to make sure."

Sophie nodded. "Did you really say that there were more of you?"

"Oh, yes. Our tunnels stretch all the way under the hill," Josephine explained, sitting down comfortably next to Sophie, and spreading out her pink skirt. "And it's a good thing too. It's very hard work. We couldn't possibly manage with any fewer of us." She waved a paw proudly across the soft green turf. "Look at it. Beautifully neat and tidy."

Sophie opened her mouth and then shut it again, looking at the grass. "You mean, that's what you do?" she asked at last. "You cut the grass?"

"Certainly we do! You don't think they could ever get a lawnmower up such a steep slope, do you? Why, it would just fall straight off!" The little guinea pig shuddered at the thought, and then peered down the hill. "It would be just like those two silly boys," she added, waving a paw at Dan and Benjamin, who were rolling over and over in a tangle of arms and legs. "The city council did send someone to cut it once, or so my great-great-great grandfather said. The poor man broke a leg, and said never again. But somehow, strangely enough, the grass here just never seems to get any longer." She winked at Sophie. "Isn't that lucky? Of course, now that there are so many visitors, we have to tidy up as well. We don't mind, though. Sometimes we find the nicest things." She looked at her pink tutu, and then up at Sophie, who said hurriedly, "Oh, yes. That ballet skirt really does suit you."

"Yummy things to eat too," Josephine said, resting a paw on her plump ginger stomach. "Lavender macarons are my favourite, from the shop across the road. Such a pretty colour. Unfortunately, people just don't drop those very often."

"I suppose not... But I thought that guinea pigs only ate grass and seeds and things."

"That would be rather boring, wouldn't it? And anyway, lavender macarons taste like flowers," Josephine said firmly. "Delicious. Of course, I couldn't manage a whole one." She looked thoughtful. "Although I could try." Then she twisted round and gasped. "Someone's coming!"

Sophie looked round too, and saw Dan, running up the balustrade towards them, arms stretched sideways to balance. "That's my brother," she started to explain, but Josephine was gone. Completely gone, disappeared, and so quickly that it was as if she had never been there at all.

Sophie sat with her mouth open, her eyes suddenly stinging with tears.

She *had* imagined it! She blinked and sniffed, and told herself that she should have known. "You are a baby," she whispered sadly to herself. "It's no wonder no one at that school likes you." She wrapped her arms around her middle, feeling chilly. It was as if the warmth had suddenly gone out of the afternoon.

After all, who would ever believe that there was a family of guinea pigs, living under the hill? It was such a silly story...

But then, that was exactly what Josephine had said. She'd stared straight at Sophie, with sparkling black eyes, and said that only the very cleverest people would ever see what she really was.

"Could I really have made it up?" Sophie whispered to herself, looking at the beautifully short, tidy grass. It did look *exactly* as though it was nibbled away to neatness every night by a family of guinea pigs...

CHAPTER TWO

"Sshhh!"

Sophie pressed her hand against her mouth to stop herself squealing, as the little ginger-and-white face popped out again from under the bush. There was a tiny arched doorway, now that Sophie looked properly. And there was a polished brown wooden door folded back underneath the stems of the bush. "Don't tell him! Promise! I shall have to see if I like him first."

"Does that mean you like *me*?"
Sophie whispered. The hard lump of
sadness that had been sitting in her
chest ever since they left their home in
England melted a bit. Someone liked
her! Someone special and funny and
sweet. . .

"Of course I do! Really, you do
ask some silly questions, Sophie. Ssshh!"
And Josephine ducked again, so that
she was just a tuft of particularly lush
green grass.

"Where have you been?" Dan
demanded, staring down at Sophie.
"Mum's looking for us."

"I've been here," Sophie said, folding

her arms. "You were the one who went running off!"

"You've just been sitting here on your own, all this time?" Dan sounded quite disgusted, and Sophie tried not to giggle.

"Not quite on my own..."

But Dan wasn't listening. "Guess what? Benjamin's mum has just been to the macaron shop across the road. She gave me one, raspberry and chocolate. It was soooo good." Dan looked at Sophie smugly, and the patch of green grass by Sophie's foot wobbled.

"Lucky..." Sophie sighed.

"I'm only teasing, Sophie." Dan held

out a paper napkin. "Look, she gave me one for you, too. Lavender. I know they taste a bit funny, but it was the only one left. Do you want it?"

Sophie peered into the napkin and sniffed the sweet, flowery, sugary smell.

"Oh, I want it! I want it!" a voice squeaked, and Josephine scrambled out from under the bush and danced up to Sophie and Dan, the grass on her hat waving madly. "Me! Me! Me!"

Dan sat down suddenly on the balustrade, his face going rather

pale. His eyebrows disappeared up into his brown scruffy hair as he stared at the guinea pig in the tutu and the grass hat, who was now sniffing dreamily at the little purple cake.

"Oh, Sophie, a whole macaron..." Josephine squeaked. "I've never even *seen* a whole macaron!"

"Break her off a bit, Dan!" Sophie said, nudging him gently with her elbow. Her brother's face looked so funny. His eyes were round, like marbles.

"What is she?" Dan whispered.

Sophie sighed, in a very grown-up sort of way. "She's a guinea pig, silly. They live here, in tunnels all under the hill.

Those funny green bushes are their front doors. Didn't you know?" She was trying so hard not to laugh at Dan's confused face. For once, she knew more about something than her big brother did. He was always making her feel useless because she was younger and didn't know things.

Dan looked as though he wanted to say that was impossible, but Josephine was sitting in his lap, eating a paw-sized chunk of lavender macaron, and letting out breathless little squeaks of joy.

"I didn't know," he said humbly, and Sophie glowed.

"Dan! Sophie!"

"That's Mum calling," Sophie said, scrambling up. "They want us back for those photos. Oh, no!" She held out the flounced lacy skirt of her dress. "Look, it's torn – I must have caught my foot in it when I fell off the steps."

"You fell off?" Dan rolled his eyes, but looked guilty when Josephine tapped his arm with one little clawed paw. "Sorry, Sophie. It's not that bad. Can't you just turn sideways a bit for the photo? No one would know."

"I'd know," Sophie said in a whisper.

"It's such a beautiful dress. Auntie Lou got it for me specially, and I love it. And Mum will be so cross."

Josephine peered over at the torn dress, and then looked at her lavender macaron rather sadly. "Oh, well. I suppose eating the whole thing might have given me the collywobbles," she sighed. Then she bounced off Dan's knee, and scurried to her front door. "Ernest! Ernest!" she hissed loudly, and Sophie and Dan looked at each other in excitement. Were they about to meet another of the guinea pigs? Trying not to be too obvious about it, they both leaned closer.

"Ernest! Hurry up and come here! I

don't care if you were asleep!" Josephine squeaked crossly. "You're far too fond of sleeping. You'll get fat. Fatter."

The voice that answered her was rumbly and dark. "Josephine! It's still light out there! What are you doing outside, you silly little guinea piglet! Someone will see you! Get back into the tunnel this minute."

"I can't, Ernest. There's someone here needing your help. Please do come out and see," Josephine pleaded. Sophie could see her whiskers quivering. "And there's a reward! A most delicious one!"

"Oh, very well," the older guinea pig grumbled. "I suppose if it's important.

Does this mean I have to wear one of those silly hats? I look foolish..."

Eventually, a dark head popped out of the doorway, and glared at Sophie and Dan. "Well? I do hope that one of you is in direst need. She woke me up for this, you know."

Even under a grass hat, it was easy to see that Ernest was a very different sort of guinea pig from Josephine. His fur exploded all over him in whirls and curls of black and white – and he also looked decidedly grumpy.

"I'm not sure if it is direst need," Sophie said, in a small, apologetic voice. "I tore my dress. But it is a very special dress, for being a bridesmaid..."

"Show me!"

Sophie held out the torn flounce, and Ernest made a little clucking sound, just like Mum did when Dan turned up covered in mud from playing football.

"What a mess. Scoot over here a bit, little girl."

Sophie nearly said something – how could he call her little, when she was at least twenty times bigger than he was? – but she held her tongue. After all, it did look like he was going to help her.

"Mmm. Yes. Not too bad. Clean edges." And the black-and-white guinea pig whipped out a needle and thread from somewhere in his fur, and started to sew up the tear. Sophie leaned towards him, watching in amazement as his neat little paws whisked over the fabric. The thread was so fine that she could hardly see it as it wove in and out. She had a feeling that he was sewing up her torn dress with one of his own white hairs.

"There." He nipped the thread with his sharp, yellowish teeth, and smoothed the fabric down.

"But ... I can't see it..." Sophie said, staring at her dress. The tear was gone — the dress looked as good as new.

"I should hope not!" the elderly guinea pig exclaimed, sounding rather offended.

"You're so clever," Sophie said admiringly, and Ernest ducked his black head shyly.

"Ah, years of practice, you know. Now, did someone mention...?"

"Here." Dan handed him a chunk of macaron, and Ernest's eyes shone with excitement. "A macaron! Fancy!" He

took it in his gnarled paws, and sniffed
blissfully. Then one of his silky ears
fluttered, and he glanced up the hill.
"Now, off you go, little girl. I have a
feeling that's your mother calling you."
And he turned and lumbered back
through the doorway under the bush,
swinging his portly bottom behind him.

"Goodbye!" Josephine
reached up and dabbed
a damp little guinea
pig kiss on
Sophie's cheek.
Sophie
pressed her
hand to her

cheek to catch the kiss, smiling. Then she looked down worriedly as Josephine scampered across the grass. "Will we see you again? Please don't go!"

"You will, I promise. Come back soon! Come and visit us!" And then Josephine darted away into the hole too, leaving Dan and Sophie staring at each other, still not quite sure what to believe. Guinea pigs? In little grass hats? Talking guinea pigs? Perhaps they had only been dreaming...

But there was a macaron on Dan's lap still, with two small chunks missing. Paw-sized chunks. Dan folded the napkin over it, and laid it carefully next to the hole. As Sophie stood up, she was sure she could see it start to move slowly inside, as though eager little paws were tugging on it.

"We will come back," Sophie whispered, as her mother came hurrying down the steps to find them. "I promise we will! We'll see you again soon. Goodbye! *Au revoir!*"

Chapter Three

Sophie woke on Monday morning to find her room glowing with golden sunlight. For the first time in ages, she didn't immediately think about school and how miserable it was. Instead she remembered Josephine's sparkling black eyes, and the silky ripples of her orange-

and-white fur. Sophie sat up in bed,
with her arms wrapped around her
knees, and thought about Josephine's
breathy little giggle, and the feel of a
small pink paw in her hand. After their
wonderful day on Saturday, she and Dan
had tried to persuade Mum and Dad to
let them go back to *Sacré Coeur*, but Dad
had already planned a day trip to the
Palace of Versailles for Sunday. Sophie
had loved it, especially the amazing
hall of mirrors – but she had imagined
Josephine twirling down the room,
a little flying figure in a pink tutu,
reflected on for ever. Perhaps she had
been there, Sophie wondered.

Did the guinea pigs ever leave their steep green hill? Were there guinea pigs all over Paris? There were so many questions she wanted to ask.

"Are you awake?" Dan was peering round her door, his hair standing on end, and pillow creases down his cheek.

Sophie nodded at him. "I was just
thinking."

Dan hurried in and sat on the end
of her bed. "It did happen, didn't it? I
wanted to talk to you all of yesterday,
but Mum and Dad were with us every
minute." He looked at her sideways, as

though she might laugh at him. "We did see them?"

Sophie smiled dreamily at him. "Mm-hm."

"We have to go back!" Dan bounced excitedly, and Sophie wobbled and then nodded. "Yes. After school. Mum won't mind, she likes sitting on the benches and watching all the people." Then she sighed a little as Dan went back to his own room to get dressed. *After* school – that meant she had to get through school first. Another day of Chloe and Adrienne giving her the side-eye and making snarky comments. She got out of bed reluctantly, and pulled a T-shirt and jeans out of the cupboard. That was the one good thing about her French school – no uniform.

Sophie's mum had photos spread over the table, dotted around in-between the breakfast plates. Sophie peered at them. "Did you print these out? Auntie Lou looks gorgeous," she said admiringly.

Her mum smiled at her. "So do you. And Dan's even looking at the camera in some of them..."

Sophie grinned. Dan was useless at having his photo taken. He was always cross-eyed or getting the giggles. She picked up the close-up portrait of her and Auntie Lou together, hugging each other, with Auntie Lou's wedding veil

streaming in the breeze behind them.
They were standing on the steps, and the
white dresses gleamed against the green
grass. "Can I have this one?" Sophie
asked, the photo
trembling a
little in her
fingers.

Her mum
nodded. "Yes,
that's a pretty
one. I could get
you a frame for
it if you like."

But Sophie

wasn't listening. In the back of the

picture, peeping from behind Auntie Lou's dress – was that a little gingery face? She was almost sure it was.

Sophie hurried through the playground, staring at her feet. She was looking for some quiet little corner where she could avoid the girls in her class until the end of morning break, but the playground was titchy, and everywhere was full. Even her favourite chestnut tree had a group of boys climbing all over it. In the end she perched on a scrap of wall between two groups of older girls, and pulled the photo out of her pocket. She'd found a little plastic folder in her bedroom, and slipped the picture inside. Now she ran her finger over it lovingly. She wanted to take a proper photo of Josephine, but this was fine for now. Besides, she didn't have to hide this picture away. Only someone who knew where to look would spot the furry little face, peering out at them.

"What's that?"

Sophie looked up, blinking, and flinched. Chloe was staring down at her. But she didn't have that superior expression on her face, and there was no sign of Adrienne, for once.

"It's my auntie's wedding," she said, clutching the photo tightly, in case Chloe should try to snatch it away.

"That's a lovely dress," Chloe said. Sophie looked at her doubtfully. But she seemed to mean it. There was a dreamy sort of look in her eyes as she admired the lacy flounces. "Did it swish when you walked?"

"Ye-es," Sophie agreed. She was still waiting for this to turn into some mean sort of game. But Chloe just looked envious. "I'd love to be a bridesmaid. I wish *my* auntie would get married. I know just what my dress would be like. I mean, yours is beautiful," she added hurriedly. "It's just that I'd love a great big bow at the back as well..."

Sophie nodded. "What colour?" she asked cautiously.

"Oh, purple. Definitely purple, a sort of lavender colour." Chloe stared blissfully into the distance, and Sophie nodded and smiled. But she was thinking of lavender macarons, and that same blissed-out look on a round guinea-pig face.

Then someone grabbed the photo, ripping it out of Sophie's hand and making her gasp.

Chloe stepped back, looking suddenly guilty and ... scared? Sophie frowned to herself. She hadn't noticed that before. Perhaps Chloe was only mean because

Adrienne made her be.

"What are you doing?" Adrienne asked Chloe sharply, pulling the photo from its plastic folder.

"Just talking to Sophie!" Chloe folded her arms, and Sophie saw her stand up straighter. Her eyes still looked frightened, though.

"We were talking about bridesmaid dresses," Sophie said. "Give me back my photo." Adrienne was clutching the picture against her top, but Sophie could still see it. She and Auntie Lou were smiling happily out of the picture – but Josephine... Sophie blinked. No, that was silly.

For just a moment, she'd thought that the little guinea pig had moved. Wasn't there more of her sticking out from behind Auntie's Lou's beautiful dress? It was almost as if she was leaning out and glaring at them. At Sophie. *She's probably trying to tell me to stand up for myself*, Sophie thought, feeling suddenly guilty.

"I'm keeping it." Adrienne smirked at her.

Sophie gaped at her. "You can't. It's mine."

Adrienne rolled her eyes. "So? You're such a baby." She stepped back, and all at once Sophie knew what she meant to do. She was getting out of Sophie's reach. Grinning, she ripped the photo in half, and in half again, on and on until it was in tiny bits. Then she threw them in the air, so they came down on Sophie like the confetti she'd thrown for Auntie Lou.

Sophie crouched down, and started to pick them up, her eyes stinging. Her lovely picture! Her special reminder of Josephine!

"Here." Someone stuffed the last little piece into her hand, and Sophie looked up. It was Chloe, her face miserable. "Sorry!" she whispered, and scuttled off after Adrienne.

Sophie looked at the scrap of paper, and sighed. It was hardly bigger than her thumbnail — but there was a tiny, furry face staring crossly at her. She had a feeling that if the piece had been any bigger, she'd have seen that now Josephine had her paws folded over her front, and that her foot was tapping crossly under her pink net tutu. The guinea pig was definitely giving her a stern look.

"I'm not very good at standing up to people," Sophie whispered. "Not even Dan, and he's just my brother. I didn't know what to do..."

And then all at once, she did know exactly what to do. She had been planning to go back to the church to see Josephine anyway. She would ask the little guinea pig for help.

Chapter Four

Sophie huddled at one side of the steps, with Josephine hidden beside her. Dan had football club after school, which he'd forgotten about, but he'd made her promise to go and find Josephine again, and to tell him *everything* later. Sophie was quite pleased that he wasn't there, to be honest. It would give her a chance to ask Josephine for advice. She had tried to talk to Dan about feeling lonely at school, and he hadn't been very sympathetic. Not because he didn't care – he just didn't understand how it felt.

Sophie had easily persuaded Mum that there was no point in going all the way home, and it would be boring to sit at school and wait for football to finish. So they could just go and sit on the benches at *Sacré Coeur*, and perhaps even buy a macaron... Mum was over on a bench at the side of the path daydreaming as she ate hers.

She eyed Josephine sideways. The

guinea pig was sitting tidily on the stone step, eating a rose-flavoured macaron, and whispering happy little hums about how delicious it was. She didn't look magical at all – for a talking guinea pig. "Did the photo actually move?" Sophie whispered.

Josephine glanced up at her, and winked. "Don't be silly, Sophie. How could it possibly?" She fixed Sophie with a stern glare. "And we have much more important things to worry about. Do I understand this correctly, Sophie? You are not enjoying being in Paris? The *grrr*eatest city in the world?"

Josephine was growling her Rs, Sophie

noticed. It made her sound extremely cross. Hastily, Sophie broke off another piece of macaron – they had run out of lavender ones, but Josephine had assured her that rose with chocolaty goo in the middle was almost as nice anyway. "Here."

The little guinea pig sniffed in delight, and stuffed the whole piece in with both paws so that her cheeks were even fatter than before. "Paris," she told Sophie thickly but determinedly, "is the nicest possible place to live."

"I know..." Sophie sighed. "But all my friends are back at home." She glanced shyly at Josephine. "I mean, apart

from you, of course. And I had to leave my cat, Oscar, behind."

Josephine sniffed, and brushed macaron crumbs out of her whiskers with fussy paws. "A *cat*, Sophie?" she said, as though she was disappointed.

"He's a very nice cat. He'd like you! He doesn't chase other animals. I mean, squirrels and things," Sophie assured her. "Not that you're anything like a squirrel," she added hurriedly, as Josephine stiffened and shot her a haughty glare.

"Those enormous fluffy tails," Josephine muttered eventually. "Quite unnecessary. So vulgar..." There was a suspicion of a sigh in her squeaky voice,

and Sophie wondered if she was a teensy
bit jealous.

"You look much smarter without a
tail," she promised. "And I think a tutu
and a tail would be too much."

"Of course it would," Josephine
snorted, but she looked happier, and
she smoothed down her tutu lovingly.
"This is all beside the point, Sophie,"
she said firmly. "I will pretend that I
didn't hear about the cat." She shuddered.
"But it doesn't matter." She laid a paw
on Sophie's knee. Sophie could feel the
delicate claws pricking through her jeans.
"I quite understand that you miss your
old home, and it's right that you miss

your old friends. But you must promise me that you won't let it spoil you being here." She waved at the view of rooftops, set against a perfect pale blue sky. She glanced sideways at Sophie, then ducked her head. "With me," she added in a whisper.

Sophie reached down and scooped Josephine into her arms, a warm, solid bundle of fur. She knew she shouldn't, but she had to. If anyone saw, they would just think that the guinea pig was a toy.

She pressed her cheek against Josephine's smooth fur.

"I promise. Of course I do. But it's hard to remember how lovely you are, and how gorgeous Paris is, when Adrienne is so horrible to me. And actually, I don't think it's just me she's mean to. Chloe follows her around everywhere, but I think that's only because she's scared of what Adrienne will say if she doesn't do as she's told."

"Hmmm..." Josephine wriggled out of Sophie's arms, and actually put down the rose macaron. "This is not good, Sophie. I am most shocked that a little French girl should be so mean. We really cannot let this go on, now, can we?"

Sophie stared at her hopefully. It ought to feel silly – a guinea pig sounding so determined, and so stern. But it didn't feel silly at all. Josephine might only be small, but there was a glint in her black eyes that made Sophie feel almost sorry for Adrienne.

"What are you going to do?" she asked.

Josephine had the macaron in her paws again, and she looked at Sophie over the top of it. "Ha!" she muttered. "Just you wait and see."

Sophie set off for school the next day

with mixed feelings. She was worried about seeing Adrienne, and at the same time cross with herself for letting the other girl upset her so much. And she was desperate to see what Josephine was going to do. She would do something – Sophie was almost sure.

All through their lessons that morning, Sophie was sure she could feel Adrienne staring at her whenever their teacher wasn't looking. Sophie tried very hard to look as though she didn't care, but the story she was supposed to be writing was awful – more crossings-out than actual words. She couldn't help worrying about what was going to happen at breaktime.

Would Adrienne pick on her again?
Should she try and talk to Chloe? Sophie
had liked her yesterday – but she wasn't
sure that she was brave enough to be
Chloe's friend, not if it meant making

an enemy of Adrienne. She wasn't sure
Chloe was brave enough, either. As the
morning went on, Sophie's strange, sweet
faith in Josephine drained away, little by
little.

When the class rushed out into the
tiny playground, Sophie felt someone tug
at her hair. She pulled away, dashing for
the corner by the old chestnut tree. It
was her favourite part of the school —
she liked to sit and read there, crouched
on the tree's thick, gnarled roots. If
only she could get round to the other
side of the tree before Adrienne spotted
where she was going, then she might be
able to hide... But because her school

was right in the middle of a big city, the playground was small. If Adrienne bothered to look, Sophie knew it would be very difficult for her to stay hidden away.

She pulled a book out of her bag and tried to concentrate on enjoying it – it was one that Elizabeth had sent her as a just-because-we-miss-you present – but she kept reading the same page over and over, and it didn't seem to be making any sense. What had Josephine meant? Was there really anything a tiny guinea pig – even a very special guinea pig – could do to stop someone so mean? Yesterday, Sophie had been sure that

Josephine would help. She had thought that everything would be all right. But just this minute, all she felt was lonely, and scared.

Then someone tugged on her hair again. Adrienne! It had to be! Sophie couldn't keep pretending not to notice. She looked round miserably, waiting for a nasty comment, or maybe a push.

But instead, looking at her from a small hollow between the great, spreading branches of the tree, was a tiny ginger-and-white face. A face that would have had a very smug smile, if guinea pig mouths were made that way.

"Josephine!"

"Ssshhh! I am undercover."

"How did you get here?" Sophie whispered. "How did you even know where my school was?"

"I followed you," Josephine said proudly. "This morning. I watched for you going to school. It isn't far. I went quite a lot of the way in the bottom of a pushchair. And then I climbed into your backpack when you got your pencil case out. I was *very* clever," she added, preening herself a little.

"What if someone had seen you?"

"Then I would have pretended to be a doll. I have it all thought out, Sophie. I must admit, I'd never realized how useful this tutu would be! It's my disguise. A real guinea pig wouldn't wear a pink tutu, would she? So it goes without saying that I can't be a real guinea pig."

"I suppose..."

"You worry too much. Now where is she, this Ad*rrrr*ienne?"

Sophie leaned out to sneak a glance around the tree trunk, and then darted back, her cheeks pale. "There! Coming towards us, oh, Josephine, I think she saw me!"

"Well, good." Josephine dusted her paws together, and then hopped down so she was half-hidden by Sophie's skirt. "After all, we can't teach her the error of her ways if we keep on hiding, can we?" Then she ducked further as Adrienne appeared, looming over Sophie, with Chloe close behind her, looking miserable.

"Are you hiding from us?" Adrienne asked, smirking.

"No. I'm just reading my book." Sophie could feel the warmth of Josephine's fur, pressed against her skirt. It made her feel brave, and her voice didn't wobble at all. "What's it to you, anyway?"

Adrienne sucked in a breath through her teeth. She wasn't used to Sophie standing up to her. Then she peered over the top of the book, and frowned. "What's *that*?"

"What?" Sophie asked, pretending to be confused. Josephine was staring back at Adrienne with her paws folded, her black eyes sparkling.

"Sophie, this girl is extremely rude. I think you're quite right not to like her," she said, glaring at the bigger girl.

Adrienne gaped at her. Then she shook her head, as if she hadn't quite believed what she'd heard, and smirked at Sophie. "Aww! You brought your little cuddly toy to school, Sophie. That's so cute..."

"I am not a toy and you know it," Josephine squeaked. "I am a friend of Sophie's, and I shall be keeping an eye on you, Mademoiselle. You are nothing but a bully!"

This time Adrienne stepped back, looking scared. "What *is* that?" she muttered. "It's creepy..." Chloe was

staring at Josephine too, but Sophie
thought she looked hopeful, rather than
frightened.

"It! It! How dare she?" Josephine
hopped on to Sophie's knees and danced
up and down with rage. "I am not
*crrrr*eepy, either! *You* are creepy, you
mean bully!"

Chloe burst out laughing. "Oh,
Sophie, who is she? She's so lovely! And
you're absolutely right." Chloe nodded at
Josephine, then she turned on Adrienne,
her hands clenched into fists by her
sides. "You *are* a bully! You are! And
I've just been too scared of you to ever
say so!"

"HA!" Josephine squeaked in triumph,
bouncing on Sophie's knees. "That's it!
You tell her!"

"Girls, what are you doing? There seems to be a lot of noise over on this side of the playground." Mademoiselle Bellerose had appeared without them even noticing – or at least without the girls noticing. Josephine had nipped back into Sophie's open bag.

"It's Sophie!" Adrienne said, colour flooding into her face. "She's got – I mean, she's brought – she's brought a pet to school!"

Sophie fought to keep the grin off her face – it was extra-hard when she could hear a tiny, disgusted "Hmf!" from inside her schoolbag.

"Sophie?" Mademoiselle Bellerose

looked at her, one eyebrow raised.

"I don't understand." Sophie shook her head. "I don't have any pets, Mademoiselle. Not here..." She let her voice wobble, just a little bit. "Back at home in England I have my cat, Oscar." Another "Hmf!" rather louder. Sophie patted the side of her bag apologetically. "But my mum said it wouldn't be fair to bring him here. He wouldn't like living in a flat in a strange place..." She gazed sadly at the teacher, and Mademoiselle Bellerose nodded sympathetically.

"Of course, of course, you poor child. Adrienne, it's very unkind to tease poor Sophie like this. You should know she's missing her cat. Go inside, please. I shall be keeping my eye on you." And she marched away, with Adrienne trailing beside her, looking confused, and a little bit scared.

"Sophie!" Chloe whispered, her eyes round and shining. "What is she? What have you got in your bag? I told Adrienne that she was a bully! I don't know how I dared! It's almost like ... magic."

"Nonsense. Why should it be magic that you were brave?" Josephine popped her head out of the bag, and pointed at Chloe.

"*You* are a very nice little girl. You may be friends with my Sophie."

Sophie went pink.

"Because I can't come to school with you every day, Sophie," Josephine whispered. "I don't even know what I'm going to say to the others, they're sure to have missed me by now. Oh well. They'll probably think I've run away to join a circus. I did say that I would, the last time I argued with my sister."

"Oh! I'll take you back on the way home," Sophie promised, looking at her anxiously. "Or maybe I could pretend to be ill? Then I could go home early and you'd be back sooner. There's the bell, we have to go in. I could tell Mademoiselle I'm feeling sick now, if you like."

Josephine patted her hand. "You're very sweet. Don't worry. Maybe the others will just think I'm still asleep. We do sleep for most of the day, you see. In fact" — she pressed a paw against her mouth to suppress a yawn — "I shall sleep in your bag until it's time to go home. Zip me up, Sophie." And she disappeared into the bottom of the bag, with little sleepy squeaks.

"Who is she?" Chloe asked, gazing at the bag, as Sophie swung it gently on to her shoulder.

Sophie bit her lip, eyeing Chloe as they walked across the playground together. Josephine's home was such a deep secret. But then, she had said she liked Chloe. And no one would believe Chloe if she decided to tell, just like Mademoiselle Bellerose hadn't believed Adrienne. She linked her arm in Chloe's, and leaned closer.

"Her name is Josephine. She's a guinea pig, and she lives with her family under the hill, at *Sacré Coeur...*"

The End

Make your own
LAVENDER SHORTBREAD

Josephine loves lavender macarons, but these little almond biscuits are really hard to make. If you're lucky enough to have lavender in your garden, you can use the flowers for cooking. Here's a slightly simpler recipe that tastes just like lavender.

INGREDIENTS:

- 90g butter (at room temperature)
- 1 tablespoon of lavender flowers, picked from their stalks (you need to find a lavender bush that you're sure hasn't been sprayed with chemicals). Or you can use 1 teaspoon of dried lavender instead.
- 50g caster sugar
- 110g plain flour

YOU ALSO NEED:

- Scales
- A mixing bowl and a wooden spoon
- A knife and a chopping board

- Cling film
- A baking tray, lined with baking parchment or greaseproof paper
- A palette knife or fish slice to help get the biscuits off the tray
- A wire rack to cool the biscuits on
- A grown-up to help with the oven

INSTRUCTIONS:

1. Weigh the soft butter in a bowl. Ask a grown-up to chop the lavender flowers finely on the board and add them to the butter. Beat them together until the butter is really soft – this gives the butter lots of lavender flavour.

2. Add the sugar and beat it in, then add the flour. Now use your hands to bring the crumbly mixture into a ball, and then knead the biscuit dough lightly until it's smooth.

3. Shape the dough into a fat sausage and wrap it in cling film. Put the dough in the fridge to firm up for about 30 minutes – this makes it easier to slice.

4. Ask a grown-up to slice the sausage into about 10 rounds, and put them on the baking tray.

5. Bake at 160°C, or 140°C for a fan oven, for about 15 to 20 minutes, until they're turning golden-brown at the edges. Ask a grown-up to lift the biscuits off the tray with a palette knife and leave them on a wire rack to cool.

6. Now you just need to sit somewhere sunny, and imagine a little ginger guinea pig telling you to hurry up with her biscuit...

Look out for more

Furry FRIENDS

adventures, coming soon!

Holly has always loved animals.

As a child she had two dogs, a cat, and

at one point, nine gerbils (an accident).

Holly's other love is books.

Holly now lives in Reading with

her husband, three sons and

three very spoilt cats.